# MY CAPTOR'S DESIRE

NOVA ANGEL

*for YOU*

# CONTENT WARNING

Click HERE or scan QR code below:

# PREFACE: KANE

I sit on the roof adjacent to Haven's apartment. She should walk through her front door at any moment. I'd followed her home from work at 5 o'clock like I'd done every day for the past year. It's easy enough to do in New York City, especially during rush hour. I'm wearing a baseball cap, sunglasses, and a sloppy outfit to ensure people don't recognize me. While busy bodies crowd the streets, it allows me to keep a close distance from her. Luckily, Haven is always none the wiser.

I make sure she enters her apartment building safely before I quickly ascend the fire escape of an old abandoned factory across the street. I bought the building shortly after Haven moved into her current apartment just in case I ever ran into squatters or troubled youth. Despite its appearance, this place is my sanctuary. I spend hours on this roof watching Haven eat, sleep, and touch herself. I will not take the chance of that time being disturbed by *anyone*.

This obsession with Haven all started when we were children. After my parents died, it was the talk of the town. "New York City elites dead from a car crash" was the headline that littered every news outlet.

"Was he drinking?"

"No, I heard the Turners liked blow."

Gossip magazines were abuzz, and the conspiracy theorists were quick to suggest foul play. Everyone had something to say about my parents' death, and no matter how much I tried, it was impossible to escape the noise.

When it came time for the funeral, people gathered in crowds to see the young heir of the Turner fortune. My family owned half of the city, and after their death, I inherited it all. I became a billionaire at the age of ten. But I didn't care about the money. I cared about my family. I was utterly alone except for the servants at Turner Manor. I was a young child mourning the death of my family, and every goddamn person in this city treated me like I was some kind of spectacle.

But not Haven, no, she stood at the metal barriers that lined the church's steps with a single red rose in her tiny hands. While everyone else shouted, she stood there in silence. And for the first time since my parents' death, I didn't feel alone. I gravitated towards her like a moth to a flame, and as she handed me the rose, there was a silent understanding between us.

I was quickly dragged away then, but I haven't stopped thinking about her since. From that moment on, I was plagued by her existence. She consumes every thought of every waking moment. Of course, I have to keep up my appearances. Hosting charity galas, attending board meetings, and expanding the Turner fortune. But underneath it all, I am tormented by desire.

By the time I was sixteen, I had discovered her identity. Haven Mathews was a year younger than me. She had a sick mother who died when she was only eighteen; her father is unknown, and she loves animals. When I was nineteen, the stalking began. I needed to see her in the flesh, not just over a screen. I had spent my youth vigorously masturbating to any new photos that she would post online. But it wasn't enough. It was *never* enough.

The stalking started off innocently. I occasionally watched Haven through her dorm window at night. But over the years, it has devolved into something much more sinister. I follow her, have all of her medical records, track her phone, bugged her apartment, keep tabs on her friends, and do my best to deter any men who show her the slightest bit of interest. I spend all of my free time consumed by Haven.

Unfortunately, I can only follow her in the mornings and evenings when NYC is at its busiest because I have the best chance of blending in. While my wealth and status permit me unlimited information and access to Haven, I still have to be careful not to be spotted in public. It is one of the more frustrating parts of being well-known. I don't have free access to roam as I might wish. That is why I started hacking into the streets, stores, and office security cameras. That way, we never have to be apart. Nonetheless, we spend every evening and morning together. After all, I have a perfect spot across her apartment with a view of every room.

I refocus my thoughts and peer through binoculars as I hear keys begin unlocking her front door through my earpiece. Haven walks through the door shortly after and immediately locks it behind her. My heart swells with pride, knowing that she takes the correct precautions to protect herself against this city's scum. I grip my binoculars tighter at the thought of someone harming her. If they did, they would never be found again. I would make them pay a much higher price than death.

Her cat Luna eagerly greets her, and I watch as a smile spreads across Haven's beautiful face. I feel her happiness seep into my bones, and my cock goes rigid. I let out a soft sigh. I've spent countless nights thinking about how those lips would feel around my hardened shaft. I begin unzipping my pants to give some relief to my painfully hard cock. It springs forth, desperate for her touch.

Haven walks towards the bathroom and, like every night before this, gets ready for her nightly shower. I zoom in with my binoculars as she peels off her work clothes from her perfectly sculpted body. It's like she's teasing me. I begin slowly stroking myself, and pre-cum seeps from my tip. Her black hair cascades down her bare back, and I pray to God that she turns around and shows me her beautiful tits. But something better happens; she bends over and pulls down her panties, flashing me her bare pussy.

"Fuck," I groan and begin pumping my cock.

It's the third time I've masturbated today. I dream about her every night: sometimes I fuck her, other times I marry her, but mainly I dream about us having a family. Then morning comes, and I am ripped away from my fantasy. It is difficult to accept the reality of her absence, especially when I am greeted with painful morning wood that I must attend to. Then, sometime around midday, my thoughts of her consume me to the point where I have to step away from work and stroke myself with her dirty panties that I steal from her apartment every week. Finally, after I follow her home, we spend some much-needed quality time together. And while she doesn't know I watch her, I can tell we both feel less lonely.

Haven turns to the side and flashes me her medium-sized breasts. Her nipples are hard and pink. I wish so desperately that I could suck and nibble on them. What do they taste like? My mouth begins to salivate, and my balls tighten as I reach closer to my climax. The binoculars shake in my hand as the other works vigorously to satiate my never-ending lust.

"Uh," I grunt as seed shoots from the engorged head of my cock and lands anti-climatically on the cement floor of the roof. I'm desperate. Desperate with the desire to see my cum coat her pretty face.

My chest heaves violently up and down, and Haven enters the shower, shielding her body from my line of vision. I put down the binoculars and run a hand over my face. I've barely found any relief. Haven is my drug, and I am an addict. Anyone who has taken drugs before knows that eventually, you stop feeling the same high. That's what's happening. I want more, no, I *need* more. At one point in time, it was enough to jack off to her photos online, but then I needed to see her in person. Eventually, I started breaking into her apartment to smell the things she touched. Her cat, Luna, greets me with equal enthusiasm like I, too, am her owner. I've spent years seeping into every part of Haven's life, but none of it is enough. It will never be enough until I have her.

I pull out a velvet box from my pocket and open it to reveal a stunning fifty carat diamond ring that belonged to my mother. I finally conclude that I will never be happy until I make my dreams a reality.

Haven will be my wife. She just doesn't know it yet. I'm sick of waiting. I'm sick of watching her life from afar. I want to be her everything like she is my everything. Enough is enough. I *will* breed her. I *will* love her. And I *will* serve her.

After tonight, she will finally be *mine.*

## CHAPTER I
# HAVEN

"*M eow.*" I awake to Luna's insistent meowing. My head is foggy from sleep, and I can barely pry my eyes open. My alarm has yet to go off. Why in the world is my cat begging for food? I shove Luna away and roll over. She knows the drill. She isn't getting fed until it is time to wake up. Still, Luna is persistent.

"*MEOWWWWWWW*," she howls like she hasn't been fed in ages.

This damn cat. I huff out a tired breath and sit up in bed to scold her, "Luna, it's not time to ea—"

My words are cut off by the sight of my flashing alarm clock. The power must have gone out last night. *Shit, shit, shit!*

What time is it? I jump out of bed and run to my dresser, where my phone is charging. "Nine-thirty? Fuck! Fuck! Shit. I'm so dead." I frantically run around my bedroom trying to find clean underwear. "Where the fuck are all my panties?"

"Ugh," I groan as I eventually find a pair. This is my first corporate job since I graduated from university. Not just that, this is my dream job. I have always been a great student, but even I couldn't believe it when the top tech firm in the city decided to hire me. I cannot, I repeat, I *cannot* screw this up. But being more than 30 minutes late is doing just that.

I grab a cold bagel that I left out on the counter the night before and begin chowing it down. In an attempt to multitask, I quickly shove all my essentials into my tote bag. I must look like an absolute mess. No time to worry about my appearance. I can do my hair and make-up on the subway.

I pride myself on my quick thinking and give myself a little pat on the back as I make my way towards my door. That is until I'm stopped by the cries of my real boss, Luna.

"*MEOWWWW.*"

"Shit, sorry, L, here." I dump a generous amount of cat food into her bowl. My plump furball swaggers to her dish, and her cries are finally silenced. Hopefully, she won't hold a grudge against me for serving her breakfast so late.

I recheck my phone, and "9:40" flashes across the screen. I groan and run through my front door. I'll need to think of a good excuse for why I'm late that doesn't include accidentally sleeping in. Andy, my boss, is a hardass. Honest to god, he thinks sleeping is for pussies.

As I lock the door to my apartment behind me, I go through a mental list of everything I need: *Keys...check, computer...check, wallet..*

Suddenly, I feel a hand wrap around my waist, and a cloth covers my mouth and nose. I begin to flail, but a husky voice whispers into my ear, "Shhh, Haven, it's okay."

My assailant knows my name, but that doesn't comfort me. I don't have a chance to fight against him before the substance-soaked cloth knocks me out and I am swallowed by a black abyss.

I AM WAKING for the second time today, but this time with a throbbing headache. I try to recall everything that happened. Being late, feeding Luna...being attacked. My head clears very quickly as I remember the last fact.

I swallow hard as I take in my surroundings. I'm in a clear box within a room filled with monitors, tech, and equipment. There is only a toilet, a few cameras, and the sleeping bag I currently lie on inside of the box. Since there is not much to explore in here, my attention is grabbed by the screens that seem to depict the inside of someone's apartment. My heart sinks to my stomach as soon as I realize that it's *my* apartment.

What the fuck is going on?

As the drug starts to wear off, my fear takes over. I quickly stand on my feet and desperately try to find an exit. My heart begins pounding, and I can't breathe. I'm in full panic mode as I come to accept the truth of my predicament: I've been kidnapped.

I pound on the clear panes of the box. "HELP!" My eyes fill with tears, and my throat starts to feel constricted as I scream, "Someone help me!"

Suddenly, one of the cameras inside of the box shifts. Someone is watching me. The realization makes me feel sick. I run desperately to the open toilet and begin expelling the bagel I had eaten for breakfast. My head throbs under the bright, sterile lighting of the box. I try to catch my breath as my head slumps into the toilet because I'm afraid I might throw up again.

To my dismay, I hear footprints approaching. I look

up to meet the eyes of my captor. My body freezes as I register who stands before me.

"Hello, Haven," he purrs.

"Kane Turner," I whisper in disbelief.

On the other side of the barrier, he crouches down beside me. He looks at me like I'm his prized possession despite being hunched over the toilet. His eyes bore into my soul, and I feel incredibly vulnerable. Between the abrasive lighting and his scrutiny, I feel akin to an animal in a zoo. After all, isn't this box my cage? I am on display for his sick enjoyment.

"Wha—why?" I can't even form a sentence. Shock has paralyzed me.

"You have no idea how long I've waited for you." He places a hand against the see-through wall. "I'm sorry about the chloroform. That stuff leaves you with a nasty headache. I would know, I had one of my servants test it on me first. It was of the utmost importance to me that you would be safe. There is nothing I would do to you that I wouldn't try first," he says as if it is somehow supposed to reassure me.

There are a few heartbeats of silence, but I can only stare in wide-eyed horror while I try to process my predicament.

"I'm sure you will start feeling better throughout

the day." He gives me a shy smile, and my shock turns into anger.

"What the fuck do you want with me? You—you kidnapped me, threw me in a box for what? For your sick enjoyment? Is this what you billionaires do? Pluck women off the street just for the fun of it?" I bang against the transparent barricade, and he takes a step back. It would seem my anger displeases him as I watch his smile quickly vanish. Good, I don't want to give him any satisfaction.

"Not just anyone, *you*," he bites out.

"Me? Me! You don't know me!"

"I know *everything* about you!" he snaps.

That takes me aback. My rage mixes with confusion and fear as I look towards the monitors displaying the inside of my apartment.

"What are you talking about?" I cry and back up towards the other side of the box. I want nothing more than to be as far away as possible from the psychopath. Sobs shudder erratically out of me, and I struggle to catch my breath.

"Haven, don't—don't fight this. You are a very important person to me. Haven..?" Kane attempts to coax me, but I can barely hear his words over my own cries. I finally bump into the other side of the box. My back slides down the wall since there is no other place to go. My fingers are tingly, and I try to make a fist with my hands to regain a normal sensation. It doesn't help. My heart beats out of my chest, and I can't breathe. I feel like I'm dying.

Suddenly, the door of my cage opens. Before I know it, Kane is by my side.

"Don't touch me, you freak!" I scream as he reaches out his hand.

"Haven, please, baby, it's okay. Shhh," he tries to coo, but it is pointless. The more he tries to soothe me, the more terrified I become.

"Fuck you! Fuck you! *FUCK YOU!* Let me go!" I scream and beat my fist into his chest, but there was no winning in this fight. Kane is much larger than me. He grabs my wrists and pins me to the ground. Before I register his movement, he straddles my hips so that I'm entirely unable to move.

"Haven, baby, I love you, but if you don't stop yelling, I swear to god I will fuck that pretty little pussy of yours until the only thing you are screaming for is my cock."

That sobers me very quickly, and my whole body stills. His threat is effective. He stares down at me, and I dare a glance down to see his swollen cock tenting in his trousers.

I let out a pathetic whimper as I submit to defeat.

His eyes soften, and his thumbs begin to caress my wrist.

"What do you want from me?" I whisper.

"*Everything,*" he declares.

I squeeze my eyes shut, trying to find some reprieve from his intense eye contact. He looks at me like he's about to devour me at any moment.

"But why? I don't—I don't know you?" I say.

"Yes, you do." As if my question is silly, he continues, "We met long ago. At my parents' funeral when you gave me that—"

"Rose," I cut him off as the memory floods my mind. My mother was obsessed with the Turners. As is the entire city. The Turners are the closest thing to royalty around these parts. They were socialites and the most powerful family in the city. Their scandals, glamor, and even their death was a spectacle. I was only nine at the time when Kane's parents died in a car crash. But even then, it felt odd that my mother, I, and hundreds of others waited outside their funeral. That was the only time I had ever seen Kane Turner.

Well, until now.

He was a sad little boy, and I felt deep sorrow for him. He had just lost his parents, and everyone treated it like it was their own personal episode of a soap opera. At the time, I couldn't imagine losing my mother.

That is, until I did.

"See, you remember." Kane reminisces and slowly lets go of my wrists, which still hold me down.

"I've been in love with you ever since that day. My parents had died, and I thought I was going to be all alone forever. But then I spotted you in a crowd of hungry wolves holding that rose." He backs off of me, and I quickly scramble into the corner of the box like a scared animal. I hold my knees tightly to my chest as he continues his twisted explanation.

"It took me a couple of years to find you. And when I did, it was the happiest day of my life. Until today, that is." He laughs to himself, and his black bangs fall into his beautiful face. The motherfucker might have kidnapped me, but there is no denying his beauty. He is New York City's most eligible bachelor for a reason. But NYC's most eligible bachelor is a recluse. He is only accessible through business and his famous charity galas which he hosts at his manor. Now I know why: the guy is totally off his rocker. But alas, his lack of public appearances only adds to his mystique.

Kane crawls over to me, positioning his body in front of mine. Even on his knees, he towers over me. There is no way I'm fighting my way out of this. I bury my face into my knees to find some reprieve from my abductor, who is dead set on encroaching on my space.

"I know that you don't really know me. But that's all going to change. That's why you are in *here*." He regards the cage that I'm in as if it's some kind of team-building exercise.

"Kane, I can't stay here. I have to go home. I have a job, a cat, and my friends!" I plead, but his demeanor quickly turns sour.

"This is your home," he growls. "When you start behaving, you can begin exploring parts of the manor, but until then, this is a necessary precaution."

"Necessary precaution? Do you hear yourself?" I shout. "You kidnapped me, and now you are keeping me in a cage! That's not...love."

"Don't ever question my love for you, Haven!" he barks and grabs my face. "Never ever question my love." His eyes are mad with rage, which frightens me. "You graduated from NYU with full honors. You are smart enough to know your dream job was too good to be true. No one directly out of college lands a gig like that. How do you think that happened, baby? *Me*. I got you that job!" he exclaims, desperate for me to understand.

"That can't be true, I-I," I stutter even though I know that it is. "Even if you got me the job, that doesn't mean you love me. Stalking is not love!"

His eyes darken. "I know how much you love animals. I know that your favorite TV show is *Grey's*

*Anatomy.* I know that you are allergic to bees. I know your favorite color is red, but not bright red; it's more of the gothic dark kind. I know that men never call you back after the first date because I pay them to never speak to you again. I know that you scrunch your nose when you are about to orgasm." Kane leans forward. "I know because I've watched you for years. I've used my power and connections to bribe doctors and lawyers to dig for any information about you. I've spent a mini fortune on real estate just so I could have the best vantage point of your apartment. Haven, don't you understand? To be loved is to be *seen*."

I stare at him in shocked silence as I reel from his confession.

"Then why am I in a cage?" I let out a ragged sob

He places his forehead against mine, and the moment feels raw and vulnerable. Kane lets out a frustrated sigh. "It's not a cage, baby. Fuck. Don't cry." He wipes away my tears with the palm of his hand. "I tried to keep my distance. I tried finding women that looked like you. I even tried to fuck them, but I could only do it if they faced away from me, and it always ended the same. With me screaming your name and then feeling disgust. I *tried*. But you are seared into my flesh and bone. I can't escape my desire for you any longer. I feel like I'm drowning without you. I've thought about all of the different possibilities for me to worm my way into your life. Still, I knew the second I came face to face with you that I couldn't control myself," he explains breathlessly.

"Haven, I'm desperate for you to know me like I know you. I can't..." He swallows. "I can't get you out of my mind. I'm sick, and you are the only cure." A rogue tear rolls down his cheek and it drops onto my lips, mingling with my own. I don't know what to say; he is right about one thing. He is sick. But maybe I'm sick too, because a small part of me wants to ease his pain. Kane's eyes plead with mine, but I clench my jaw tighter rather than give him a response. I can't show him how his words affect me. I refuse to fall victim to his haunting gaze.

Kane lets go of my face and stands suddenly, composing himself. Despite my better judgment, I feel his body's absence keenly. He might be my captor, but his presence anchored my panic. Feeling exposed again, I hug myself even tighter.

"I will give you time to settle in," he declares coldly, and all the desperation from his confession is gone. He doesn't turn around as he leaves me, making it clear that my reaction to his declaration upset him. He makes his way to a set of silver doors that opens into an elevator. I remember his words from earlier: *"If you behave I will let you explore the manor.*" I must be underneath the Turner manor then.

As he exits the room, my mind races with everything that has happened since this morning. A few hours ago, my biggest issue was being late to my big tech job. Now, I'm the captive of the most powerful man in New York City. I weep in the lonely solitude of my transparent cage as I come to terms with my predicament. Kane Turner is my stalker, and more frighteningly, he wants more; he wants my heart.

## CHAPTER 2

# KANE

"Breakfast, Mr. Turner." Agatha, the manor's housekeeper, brings forth a silver tray full of waffles and bacon. Haven's favorite.

"Excellent. Thank you, Agatha. I will bring it to Haven. Maybe this will lift her spirits."

"Patience, Mr. Turner. She will fall in love with you soon enough," Agatha reassures me, and for that, I am grateful.

I take the tray from my loyal servant's hands and head towards the elevator. The anticipation of seeing her in the flesh this morning has my cock hardening. It was already difficult enough to keep my hands off of her yesterday. I've attempted to relieve myself multiple times in the night, but it was unsuccessful. She has spent the last twenty-four hours weeping as I watched her through the bunker's cameras. Contrary to what Haven might think of me, I have never been turned on by her pain. She doesn't know how badly I wanted to comfort her. I spent the night restless as I helplessly watched her struggle. I debated going to her countless times, but Agatha assured me her mood was sour each time she delivered a meal.

I let out a sigh. All I want to do is hold her, stroke her hair, and tell her everything will be okay as long as she is with me. But alas, she made her feelings towards me known. Haven hates me, and I feel her rejection keenly. I would give her everything. I *have* given her everything. Why doesn't she see that?

I ultimately decided to heed Agatha's warning and stay in my bedroom. I have not seen Haven since yesterday's encounter. It's the longest I've gone without seeing her in years. Partially to give her time to settle in, but mainly because I don't trust myself around her. I need to know what her flesh feels like. To touch it, caress it, be inside of it...

My mind wanders to a dark place. It is not enough that she accepts me. I want to devour her. A thought crosses my mind; I could always force her to submit to me and, hopefully, place a baby inside of her womb. Surely a child will make her fondness for me grow.

But the thought is dashed as quickly as it came. I

couldn't. Any child of mine will be born out of mutual love. I can't bear the thought of Haven's wails as I relentlessly impale her with my cock. No matter how deeply I desire her.

I shake my head, attempting to refocus my mind away from the unsavory thoughts. No, the only screams from Haven when I am fucking her will be those of pleasure. Still, I don't know how long I will last until I reach my limit.

Hopefully, this breakfast surprise will cheer her up. We haven't started out on the right foot, but that doesn't mean she can't learn to love me as I love her.

The elevator doors slide open, and I straighten my spine; I need to gather my composure.

My mind troubles me as I descend down to the bunker. This space underneath the manor has existed long before me. Although, I was the one who made a few upgrades to the tech and furnishings. I had the large square enclosure installed soon after I started stalking Haven. I had initially built it for any of her persistent suitors who decided to take my bribe and still attempted to see her. Luckily for them, the greedy cowards all heeded my warning. Only proving they never deserved her in the first place.

Maybe I always knew in the back of my mind that it

would end up like this. That eventually, I would be driven mad by my desire for her until I couldn't take it anymore. There were so many times over the years where I thought about our current reality. But each time I deterred myself. I wanted to be a better man for Haven. Sadly, I am not.

The silver doors open, and I see Haven sitting in the corner of the box, playing with her hair. I shake off the doubts in my mind and focus on the task at hand. Will she notice that I've gone out of my way to make her a favorite breakfast? Thankfully, I can see that, while her eyes are still puffy, she has stopped crying. Although she doesn't seem too happy to see me.

"Hi, baby. I brought you breakfast." I give her a gentle smile, but I am met with her cold stare.

"I'm not hungry."

My nostrils flare, but I keep my anger buried. I open the door to the enclosure, stepping in. Surely the savory smell will change her mind.

"I made waffles and bacon." I point towards the platter. "Your favorite."

"Unless you are here to let me out, I don't want anything from you."

My blood boils. How can she be so ungrateful?

"You need to eat," I bite out.

"I said..." She rises slowly to her feet. "I'm. Not. *Hungry*."

She is challenging me, and my first reaction is to smash the plate against the ground. But I won't let my anger get the better of me. So I place the food gently on the floor. "It will be waiting for you when you are ready."

Her eyes soften slightly. She is clearly surprised by my reaction. The flame of her ire will eventually die out as long as I don't fuel it.

She fumbles with her hands, trying to find the right words for a response. After a few moments, she finally mutters, "Thank you."

It would seem I have won this battle. I reach out to caress Haven's cheek, but she flinches away from me. I close my eyes and reassure myself that her affection will grow. Even if that is true, her reaction still pains me. I pull away my hand and make my way towards the exit completely deflated. Nothing will be accomplished right now.

"That's it?" Haven calls out just as I am about to close the door.

"What else is there?" I ask incredulously. Does she want me to stay? She hesitates to respond. Clearly, she hasn't thought through her response. "Are you just gonna leave me down here forever?"

"That is entirely up to you, Haven," I answer honestly.

We share a few silent moments until she turns away from me. Almost as quickly as I arrived, I was leaving. Although, a few minutes ago, I would have deemed this a failure, her hesitance towards my departure has given me hope. Still, it doesn't make my exit any easier. My heart aches with every step that I take away from her.

I CHECK in on Haven from one of the monitors while I work in my office. She decided to eat breakfast around noon and has since been pacing around the box. It has been nearly impossible to focus on my tasks. Every single moment, I watch her every movement just to see what she might do next. I can't believe she is finally home...with *me*. My thoughts quickly turn dirtier as I imagine fucking her on all fours in that enclosure. I want her to scream my name while I come inside her.

My cock bulges against my trousers, and I have no choice but to attempt once more to relieve myself. Having her so close and yet being unable to satiate myself is a burden I didn't think I would struggle with. I open my desk drawer and find a stash of her dirty underwear. I pluck out the first one I see and pull it close to my face.

"Fuck," I groan and begin unzipping my pants. I can't wait to finally bury my face into her pussy. I stroke my shaft slowly, and her musky scent fills my nostrils. I look towards the monitor and, like I've done for the thousandth time, I begin jacking off to her. My erection is painful, and pre-come dribbles down my shaft, creating a slippery surface, which I stroke. My eyebrows furrow, and sweat begins to coat my temples. I feel the desire for Haven in my bones, but no matter how hard or fast I stroke, I can't bring myself to completion. I'm determined to get mild relief, so I push forward, pumping my cock. I take in a deeper inhale of her dirty panties as I watch her sit in the box of my own design. But nothing happens. I can't come. She has broken me.

"Fuck!" I scream and slam the monitor against the wall. My sexual frustration is finally boiling to the surface. I can't find any relief with myself. I'm being driven mad.

I desperately uncork a bottle of whiskey and pour myself a generous glass.

*Knock knock knock*

"Mr. Turner?" Agatha's voice calls out from behind the door. She knows better than to barge into my office. I tuck my stiff cock back into my trousers.

"Come in, Agatha," I call and begin rubbing my throbbing temples.

She opens the door and looks at me with concern. "Is everything okay, sir?

"Yes, yes, it's fine," I grit out, but the smashed monitor and oncoming headache suggest otherwise.

"Oh. Well..." She searches to find the correct words. I'm not easily calmed by others. I've always been this way, ever since I was a child.

"In other news, the cat has arrived." She decides not to comment on the present situation and instead redirects my troubled thoughts.

"Luna!" I exclaim, and I am grateful for Agatha's intervention. "Where is she? Haven will be so happy to see her."

A smile creeps across my face as I think of her reaction. Haven absolutely adores the furball, as do I.

"She is waiting in the foyer, sir." Agatha walks behind me as I eagerly strut down the hall. "A servant had a difficult time capturing the creature. He sustained a few scratches."

"Ah yes, Luna doesn't like strangers." I smirk, realizing she has much in common with her owner.

"As it would seem," Agatha mutters. "Is there anything else, sir?" The poor woman tries to keep up with my long strides.

"No, thank you, Agatha. That will be all. You are dismissed."

I cannot contain my excitement. I have another excuse to see Haven and another chance of getting her to fall in love with me.

# CHAPTER 3
# HAVEN

I pick at an open cuticle of my nail. I'm alone in my cage with nothing but my thoughts. Who would've guessed being a captive is so dull.

With no clock and zero exposure to the sun, I have no idea how much time has passed since I first arrived. My three daily meals are the only thing grounding me in the structure of a normal day. Agatha, Kane's servant, brought me lunch a while ago. She is nice enough, although I can't say the same about myself. Turns out I'm a bitch when I get kidnapped. Give a girl a break.

It is even more infuriating that everyone in this godforsaken manor is at Kane's beck and call, and he has their unwavering loyalty. I mean, how many people are okay with keeping a woman trapped in a bunker until she falls in love with her captor? It would seem more than I had expected.

I begged Agatha to help me escape the first few times she delivered my food, but she only reassured me that Kane is a good man. Ugh, good man, my ass. More like a *psychopath*. A psychopath I am now hoping will deliver me my next meal so that I at least have someone to talk to. I scrub my face with the palms of my hands. What the hell is wrong with me? I can't be so weak that a couple days of boredom is making me desire the attention of a man responsible for my being here.

The one consolation prize is that all the food served in this place is my favorite. Kane arrived this morning with a platter of waffles and bacon, which was both endearing and infuriating. On the one hand, it was a reminder that Kane had spent the last four years stalking me; on the other, it was nice that a man remembered something I liked for once. But he only stayed briefly after we exchanged a few harsh words. It's odd, all of this effort, and he has yet to spend more than thirty minutes with me. I didn't peg him as the type of man who gives up at the first sign of rejection. Then again, I don't know him at all. Something I need to rectify quickly if I have any chance of escaping.

I try my best not to dwell on thoughts about him,

but I'm failing miserably. I stare at the elevator doors, waiting for him to exit them.

I blow out a long slow breath to steady my nerves. I need to get out of this box. I think I'm slowly losing my mind. But just as I try to quell the thoughts of Kane, I hear the elevator ding.

My heart skips a beat, and I jump to my feet. Eagerly awaiting some company. I'm not proud of my reaction, but boredom will do crazy things to someone's mind. I guess I really am that weak.

The elevator doors open, and Kane emerges with something black and fluffy in his hands. My eagerness quickly turns to fright as I register what, or who, he is holding.

"Luna." I whisper her name as fear grips me. If my fierce cat is not putting up a fight, then something is very wrong. My stomach lurches, and I can feel my face pale.

"Luna!" I bang on the transparent wall of the box. "What did you do to her!?" I shout and feel tears forming in my eyes. *He wouldn't.* No, if he loves me like he says he does, then he wouldn't have hurt her.

"What did I do to her? You should be asking what Luna did to the poor servant who tried to catch her." Kane coos at Luna like she is the sweetest baby in the whole wide world. As he walks closer into view, I can see that she is not visibly harmed at all. In fact, she is...purring.

My eyebrows scrunch in confusion as I witness my anti-social cat slut herself out for my captor.

I stare in disbelief. "But—"

"Luna and I have had plenty of time to get to know each other over the years. Isn't that right?" Kane scratches her underneath her chin. Her favorite spot. She responds by giving him a few licks on his nose.

"Traitor," I whisper.

That earns me a laugh. "Even your harshest critic loves me."

"So it would seem." I squint accusingly at my furry feline. I've never seen her like anyone other than me. Quite honestly, I don't know how I feel about it.

Kane opens the door to my enclosure, and his presence feels like it takes up the whole room. I forget just how large the man is. There's no place to hide in this box, and I don't fully trust myself to be near him.

I fiddle with the hangnail I created earlier and welcome the sharp, prickly pain. Kane watches me sharply, but as he enters, he doesn't encroach on my space any further. Instead, he waits for me to come to him. Somehow, that's even worse.

Only a few heartbeats pass before I bridge the gap between us, extending my arms for Luna. The truth is

I'm so happy that she's here. Finally, I won't spend my days in complete solitude.

"My angel!" I exclaim in my most annoying baby voice, pulling the creature into my arms.

"*Purrrrrrr.*" Luna rubs her face against mine. It would seem she still loves me. I can't stop my smile as I bury my face into her furry coat.

My soft-spoken manner disappears when I look back to give Kane my coldest stare. I'm not over him winning over my cat. I need at least one ally but it seems like I am fresh out of luck.

"If your looks could kill," Kane muses, but it's clear he isn't intimated.

"Then you'd be dead and I could finally get out of here," I bite out

"Oof—then it's a good thing they can't."

"Hmm," I grunt and will myself to move to the opposite side of the box.

Kane grabs a chair and drags it into the space, ensuring to lock the door behind him before he sits down.

"Why even bother locking it if you are going to be guarding it anyway?" I criticize

"You can't be too sure. After all, you have taken a self-defense class before."

"How do you know—" I stop myself from finishing

that question. Right, he knows everything about me.

"Yeah, well, lucky for you I wasn't very good at it."

"Don't say that, I think you could be rather good if you just stick with it," he says smugly.

"Okay, I'll bite. How could you possibly know how well I performed in that class? You are Kane Turner, surely someone would notice if you were in the *girls only* class," I say, exasperated. Kane turns and points to the various security monitors that line the bunker. "I didn't have to be there. I can hack into any security system in the city."

"Ugh!" I groan and Luna bumps her head into my chin looking for my attention. She really doesn't care about the dire situation we are in right now.

"So you know *everything* about me but I know nothing about you. How is that fair?" I propose the question trying to gain some more insight on my captor.

Kane lets out a breathless laugh. "You're right. It's not. So, what do you want to know?"

"Well...I—" I stutter. To be honest I haven't really thought about it. I look down and see an empty breakfast plate of waffles and bacon. "What is your favorite breakfast?"

Kane laughs in earnest this time. What a stupid question! Favorite breakfast? How could that possibly help me escape?

"Eggs and bacon."

"Hmm, boring," I muse

"Boring?" He feigns offense

"Yes!" I point my nose in the air like I have some air of authority while being locked in a cage.

A smile grows on Kane's perfectly sculpted face, and I feel my knees weaken. His eyes are soft as he gazes at me. Almost like I'm his everything.

I turn around and face the opposite side of the box, and Luna nuzzles into my chest as if to comfort me. I need to break eye contact with this motherfucker before I do something that I regret.

I hear Kane begin to exit the box, and I turn around in fear that he is already gone.

"Wait..." I call out to him before I can think better of it, and he freezes. Silence consumes the space while he waits for me to make the first move. Against my better judgment I place Luna on the floor and she saunters off to lay on my makeshift bed of blankets.

"Thank you," I whisper, "for Luna."

"Of course, Haven," Kane declares and slowly reaches out his hand to caress my cheek. "Whatever you want. You just have to ask."

I stand completely still and tell myself that going along with his advances might make him happy enough to let me go. But deep down, I know something more sinister is brewing. Some kind of twisted desire to seek comfort in his touch.

His fingers brush across my face, and I try my best to stop a shudder from rolling down my spine. His eyes bore into my soul, promising to devour me, and for a split second, I want to be served on a silver platter. Our eye contact doesn't break, and the world feels like it is moving in slow motion. I don't know when he started standing so close to me...or when he placed his hand on my hip. The gap between us is suddenly getting smaller and smaller...

"*Meowwww.*" Luna's demands for attention break the trance. I take many steps back to create distance between us. Clearing my throat, I try to regain control of the situation. Just because he brought me my cat doesn't negate the fact that he fucking kidnapped me. I need to seriously get my shit together.

"What if I want you to let me go?" I propose, trying to set my mind back on the real goal: getting the fuck out of here.

"Haven..." Kane closes his eyes in frustration. "Anything but that."

"Fine," I grind out. It was worth a shot.

"I want..." I think about my options, and if I'm going to be stuck in here, I can at least advocate for some items that will make me less bored. "A puzzle."

"A puzzle?" Kane raises an eyebrow in confusion.

"Yes. A puzzle." I lift my chin in the air to reinforce my command. Of course, Luna does her best to undermine me, headbutting my legs again.

"And I want some books."

"Okay. I can have Agatha bring you all of those things."

"Good," I announce, trying to reclaim some of my autonomy. A few moments of silence pass before Kane asks, "Is that everything?"

"What about some new clothes...?" I try to keep the conversation as neutral as possible.

"I'll have a servant pick up the latest Saks catalog. You can pick out whatever you like."

"It doesn't need to be fancy." I suddenly feel guilty at his offer to purchase expensive items. "I've just been wearing the same clothes since the other morning, and I don't want to smell. But I don't need a bunch of things. You can just get the clothes from home—" I'm rambling, but thankfully, Kane cuts me off.

"Haven," he chuckles, "I will fetch your clothes from your apartment if that's what you like, but I expect you to treat yourself. There is no expense I wouldn't spare for you."

"Fuck you," I blurt out, and my aggression shocks

both of us. His manners are...infuriating! I'm sick of him being so nice to me.

"Whoa," he laughs and puts his hands into the air like he is begging not to be shot, "I didn't realize you hated being spoiled. As far as I can remember, you like very nice things—"

"I'm serious, Kane. Stop. I can't—" I wring my hands in frustration."Stop being so nice!"

"Okay. I am sorry for being...nice?" he drawls and slowly strolls towards me.

"You kidnapped me. You are keeping me captive." I start listing out the things that have happened in the past forty-eight hours to emphasize my point but also to remind myself of everything he has done. "Just because you brought me my cat and want to buy me nice clothes doesn't mean all of this isn't fucked up!"

"I never said it wasn't fucked up, baby. All of this"— he motions towards the box—"is certifiably insane. You don't think I know that? But these are the lengths I would go to for you. I don't want the love that forces people to settle. The love that fizzles out after six months. Or the love that causes people to be complacent. I want this, in every fucked up way imaginable, as long as it ends with you being my wife."

He hovers over me, and I lose the ability to breathe.

"Stop making it hard to hate you," I whisper breathlessly

"But I don't want you to hate me." He leans down and whispers into my lips.

"Ugh—" I growl, but he silences me with a deep kiss. My body betrays me as I feel my panties moisten and my core tighten. Hate turns to lust and I bite his lip.

"Shit!"

"Fuck you!" I scream and his mouth is back at mine. I hate the way he makes me feel. I hate the way he knows me. I hate that his lips feel so good on mine.

"Yeah, baby? You promise?" he taunts me and places my hand on his rigid cock bulging in his pants.

He's fucking massive.

"Oh, that's what you want? For me to touch your big dick?" I seethe and decide to lean into the absurdity of the situation. I kneel down and unzip his trousers until his thick member springs forth. He is now completely exposed to me, but he has no shame. He stands with utter confidence as I roughly grip his shaft and shove it in my mouth with no tenderness or care. "Or is this what you want?" I mumble around him.

Kane growls and shoves my head further down his shaft. I hate myself for the increasing pleasure I feel in between my legs. Drool pools underneath me as I continuously gag on him. There is nothing loving in this interaction. I hate him. I hate him. I *hate* him...

"Mmm...it makes you so fucking hard thinking about watching m,e doesn't it. Doesn't it, you sick fuck?" I mumble.

"You know it, baby. Just like I know you would always put on a show for me." He grabs my throat and squeezes. Fuck, it's so hot. "Admit it. You might not have known I was there but you secretly hoped I was. That someone watched while you fingered your pussy until satisfaction."

"Yes!" I scream and I hate myself. Shame washes over me but also makes me wetter. The idea of him watching me while I touched myself during all those years is only turning me on further. He picks me up and I let out a squeak. He brings us over to the chair and sits down. I hover over his throbbing cock but refuse to make the first move.

"Come on, you fucking pussy, fuck my cunt. You know you want to. Think of all of those years you wanted it to be your cock that was fucking me instead of the college—AHH!" I scream as he impales me.

"You're mine. Do you understand me? *Mine!*" he growls and chokes me to the point I can't breathe. His eyes are wild and I know I've struck a nerve. He might have deterred most men in my adult life, but I'm not a virgin.

"Say it! Say it!" he yells.

"Never," I croak, and I feel my body losing some consciousness. The feeling mixed with his rough thrusts sends me over the edge. My body begins to shudder and shake with the buildup of pleasure.

"Are you going to come all over your stalker's cock?" he taunts, which brings me closer to an orgasm. This is so wrong, so why does it feel so good? Kane loosens his grip on my neck but doesn't stop his relentless thrashing into my cervix.

"Fuck, Haven. I am going to come in your pussy. How do you like the sound of that? I'm going to spill my hot seed in your cunt until you are sufficiently breeded," he moans.

"Ahhh!" I scream in ecstasy as his words send me over the edge. I feel his load shoot inside me and to my own shame, my pussy completely milks him dry. Our screams mingle together and I collapse in his arms. We both try to catch our breath and I am mortified by my actions. Worst of all, I fucked a man who is only going to leave me to rot in this prison.

I hate him, I hate this fucking box, but most of all I hate myself.

## CHAPTER 4

# KANE

Nothing but the sound of our heavy breathing fills the bunker's air. Haven stares off into the distance while laying limp against my chest. I imagine her mind is reeling after what just took place. The combination of her lust and hatred only made me want her more. While the circumstances of our relationship have deeply disturbed her, they have also turned her on. I am all too familiar with the feeling. I could never explain my obsession with Haven. I knew something was wrong with me, but eventually, I learned to accept it. I allowed my darkest desires to consume me, and look where I've ended up. With the object of my desires screaming for my cock.

Perhaps acceptance is key. After all, I just had the best fuck of my life. Despite Haven's current absent-minded state, I feel the sick satisfaction of completion. I've waited years to breed her pussy. No one, not even Haven's rejection, can ruin this moment for me.

My cock begins to soften and slowly slides out of her cum-filled cunt. The slippery white substance trickles down her thighs and back onto my semi-rigid member. We need to get her cleaned up before my dick returns to his hardened state and we start fucking like rabid animals all over again. I kiss Haven softly on the shoulder and caress her back, but my touch elicits no response. Still, she stares blankly at the wall. I internally groan. I don't care how long it takes. She will accept me even if that means I have to break in her pussy with my dick every night.

"Hey," I whisper, "let's get you cleaned up."

She doesn't respond or fight me as I lift her from my lap and hold her in my arms. I pick up my now wrinkled dress shirt off the ground and drape it over her exposed pussy. While I revel in the sight of her, it belongs only to me. No one else will have the privilege of seeing this pussy ever again.

I exit and head towards the elevator doors. She needs a bath. After everything we shared, she deserves it. Whether Haven likes it or not, she is opening up to me in more ways than one. Soon, she will be wholly mine, in body and in spirit. The doors close, and soon enough, we ascend to the manor's third floor.

*Ding.*

*Ding.*

*Ding.*

The elevator dings as we pass each floor until it finally comes to a stop. I take a peek around the corner to make sure there are no servants in the hallway. Once the coast is clear, I feel comfortable carrying Haven to my—*soon to be our*—bedroom's bath chamber. Although her mental distance after sex doesn't surprise me, her apathy toward leaving the bunker does. Surely, she will have to say something?

Perhaps I am just anxious to impress her with my home. It has been in my family for generations and is disgustingly ornate. Gothic architecture means grand ceilings, pointed archways, and stained-glass windows. This property is located just outside the city and is in a world of its own. But for the past twenty-three years, this place has been my sanctuary from the world's harshest realities. I want my family's home to be as comfortable for her as it is for me. Haven didn't grow up with much money, which can mean her reaction could go either way. Either she will be impressed, or she will hate it. If it is the latter, then I will be crushed. But I would bulldoze this place to the ground in a heartbeat as long as it meant she was happy.

By the time we enter the bath chamber, she has yet to make any observations for herself. Instead, she just blankly stares straight in front of her. I place her down on the marble countertop so I can start to tend to the bath. She wraps her arms around her body, and for a split second, I let myself believe she misses my presence. Perhaps I am just projecting my own feelings onto her unreadable expressions.

I shift away from her and turn the silver knob of the two-person bathtub. Warm water begins flowing from the spout in a rhythmic melody. As the tub fills, I start searching through cabinets for some kind of bubble bath. Normally, Agatha or one of the servants would draw my bath, making me woefully unprepared to pamper Haven.

Finally, I open a cabinet door, and I am met with the sight of Floris rose bath essence and Dr. Teal's bubble bath. Floris, I am familiar with, but I can't help but smirk at the sight of the gaudy purple Dr. Teal's bottle. However, I am happy that Agatha followed my instructions to purchase Haven's favorite soap. My cock begins to harden once more as I think back to the memory of Haven bathing in her small city apartment after a tough day at work. The way she caressed her body like she was putting on a personal show for me.

I shake my head to refocus on preparing the bath and grab both bottles. Haven looks onward as I pour soap from each container under the hot water. Soon, it will be a calming, bubbly oasis.

"Let me grab these." I slide off her silver rings and slip them into my pocket. "We don't want them getting wet. Do we?" I give her a slight smile but she doesn't pay me any attention. Oh well, makes stealing her rings easier. This way, my jeweler will be able to size the engagement ring to fit Haven. I want her to feel the satisfaction of the ring sliding onto her finger with ease and precision knowing that it will represent the future of our marriage. Nothing can be short of perfection when it comes to my girl.

"Okay, in you go." I place a quick kiss on her head and pick Haven up off of the sink counter before setting her gently into the water.

"God," Haven sighs as the warm water relaxes her tense muscles.

"Feel good?" I chuckle, and she nods her head.

I am tempted to get in the tub with her, but I know how it will end. With her riding my cock and screaming my name. Hell, maybe the warm water would help train her tight asshole to start opening up to my thick member. But even someone as sick as me knows she is not ready for that...yet.

Instead, I grab a nearby loofah and, while kneeling over the tub, I use the suds to wash her back. She moans, indicating her enjoyment, and I can see my angel returning to life. Still, I can't fully explain her sudden silence. Of course, I know she feels ashamed for her actions, but there is something more, something she isn't telling me.

I close my eyes in frustration. I want nothing more than to release her from that bunker, but I can't until she learns to accept there can be nothing left unsaid between us. I feel the engagement ring burning a hole in my pocket. Only when she is thoroughly broken in can I make her my wife and let her roam these halls freely. Ha, *freely*. Even I know that word is a joke. Haven will never be free as long as I am alive, even as my wife. I will always be there, lurking in the shadows.

"What is it, baby?" Hm?" I ask, rubbing her back with my bare hands. I dropped the loofah as soon as she was adequately cleaned, desperate once more to touch her skin. Like I said, I am an addict, and she is my drug.

She forms a line with her lips and avoids eye contact. Oh, now this is a very dangerous game she does not want to play with me. I despise secrets.

"Haven..." I use a stern voice and grab her chin so

she is forced to look at me. But as soon as I meet her eyes, I recount everything that has passed between us since I fucked her. Her general lack of protest, which was undoubtedly unlike her, her limp body leaning against mine, her arms wrapping around her body as soon as I broke contact...

"Haven, baby, you didn't think I would...leave you, did you?" I ask hesitantly. Surely, that can't be the reason. Haven's eyes immediately begin to well with tears, and her lower lip begins to quiver.

"Aww shh, baby, don't cry, it's okay." I try to soothe, but my heart is about to implode, "Haven..." I wipe away a rogue tear with my thumb. "I will never leave you. *Never*. Especially not after sex."

"Do you miss them?" she asks, diverting the conversation.

"Who?" Her question catches me off guard.

"Your parents."

"Oh. Them." I never talk about my parents to anyone, not even Agatha. Not because I don't miss them, I miss them every goddamn day, but I'm also angry at them for dying. But then I feel guilty for my anger. I don't know how to describe how I feel so I just respond with, "Yes. I do."

"I can't imagine what it was like. You know I still think about the day I first saw you. And I definitely know you still think about that day," she chuckles, and I splash her gently with the water. It feels good to know I made her smile.

"The press were awful to you and you were so young."

"Yeah well...I guess it comes with the territory of being a Turner."

"Well if I was a Turner, I would tell them to fuck off." Haven smiles at me but doesn't realize what she just replied. My mother's ring feels like it is burning a hole in my pocket and I want to tell her she will be a Turner very soon. Instead, I choose to give her a sweet smile. I am enjoying our moment and I don't want to overwhelm her. But I should get the ring size adjusted as soon as possible.

"I miss my mom too, but can I tell you something?" she whispers, looking up at me through her lashes.

Anything."

"I felt...relief when she died. I know it's awful but she was so sick that it felt cruel that she was forced to live. All of the chemo, medication, hospital stays. No one deserves to live like that."

"That's not awful, that's mercy. Your mother finally found peace and you found your freedom."

"Yeah..." she whispers and glances away.

For the first time since stalking Haven I feel guilt

eating away at me. But even I know I am too selfish to let her go. So I try to shake away the foreign feeling and begin massaging her shoulders.

I see some of the tension in her shoulders finally relax, and I lean in to kiss her softly. She doesn't reject me but doesn't eagerly respond like she did earlier.

Despite the significant progress that we've made, something nags me in the back of my mind that she isn't ready to fully accept me. It doesn't matter how many times I give her an orgasm or cum inside of her raw pussy. She will always excuse her enjoyment at the cost of my advances. For as long as I initiate intimacy, she will never have to take accountability for her reciprocated desire. Hopefully, all that will change after a nice bath and a few more days in the bunker.

I realize what must be done. I will continue to spend my free time with Haven but I will not touch her. No, only until she begs to be mine will I propose. I send up a silent prayer to god to give me strength. After tonight, I am going to need it more than ever.

## CHAPTER 5

# HAVEN

"*MEOWW!*" Luna screeches at me for more food.

"Agatha already brought your breakfast *and* lunch, you little porker." I crouch down and give her a few pets. I look up and stare anxiously at the elevator. It is usually Kane who brings his girls' food. In fact, the only time we have been apart these past few days was either after I fell asleep or when he would bring down our meals.

Why is today any different? Agatha seems nice enough, but she is not who I wish to see. Did something happen to him?

My mind goes through a million possibilities, but I assure myself that Agatha would have let me know if something happened. Or at least, she would have shown some concern. It is apparent she loves him like he is her own son.

Although I try to calm my nerves, I can't help but pace around this *stupid* box prison. I think back to all of the time we've spent together. It freaks me out to be alone for this long. And while it was initially unsettling how much he knows of me, I've gotten a lot of enjoyment from prying out information about him. Funny enough, he isn't much of a sharer. It would seem he expects that from everyone else and shouldn't have to reciprocate. And while he is reluctant to talk about himself, I get the impression that I know more than most do. He loves the color blue, he is a bit of a clean freak, his favorite breakfast is eggs and bacon, and according to him, I am his favorite person in the world.

I smile and bite at my thumbnail, thinking how, in a twisted way, it is special that he feels comfortable around me. Ugh, this is just making me want him more. I let out a frustrated whine. Perhaps I'm just sexually frustrated. Kane hasn't touched me since we last had sex, and while I initially felt ashamed for giving in to my primal desire, I haven't been able to stop thinking about it. It was like he knew my body better than I do. Every touch, every moan, every stroke, which I claimed to hate but desperately craved. And afterward, when I felt like a shell of myself, he made sure to tend to my every need.

I even got a glimpse of the famous Turner manor, and it was more beautiful than I could have ever imagined. It felt like I had been transported back in time to some kind of European castle. The house was unlike anything in New York City outside of some of the churches.

I guess it made sense; the Turners were the closest thing that the city had to royalty. It's weird; I always thought I would feel like an outsider to this kind of world. I didn't grow up with this kind of wealth. I didn't know my father, and by the time I was a teenager, I was taking care of my dying mother. It wasn't until Kane carried me in his arms through his stunning home that I realized how desperately I wanted to be cared for. I've spent my entire life taking care of someone else or myself. I wasn't intimidated by his power or influence like I thought; instead, I craved it. I felt...safe. And for a split moment in time, while I sat in a clawfoot bathtub, I didn't feel like his prisoner. I felt like his...*equal.*

I close my eyes tightly and try to take a deep breath. If he is so in love with me, why hasn't he touched me like that since? Sure, he always makes a point of being near me; stroking my back, playing with my hair, or caressing my thighs. He always gives me a peck on the lips when he arrives and when he leaves, but that is it. I've gotten so desperate that yesterday I tried sitting on his lap, and while I could feel his rigid cock against my back, he didn't make a move!

I try to get a hold of my senses. I should be focusing on escaping this box, but instead, I am worried about my captor's true intentions. I let out a long, slow breath to try and steady my thoughts. The truth is...I miss him. Something changed after he claimed me. It feels like I have wagered a sacred part of my body that I will never give back.

"Ugh!!" I groan and slap myself in the face. What the fuck is wrong with me?

"*Meoow*." Luna rubs against my leg as if she knows I need a distraction. I welcome her embrace; without her, I would have gone crazy by now.

*DING.*

The elevator arrives, and I perk up far too optimistically for my liking. I need to keep my wits about me so I can at least scold him for his absence. Although, he probably has a good explanation. Kane has made it a point that I come first.

The silver doors open, and my heart sings when I catch sight of Kane. He is tall, well-groomed, and dashingly handsome. My mind immediately begins undressing him, and my panties start to moisten. Fuck. I am so weak. But I can't help it. I *need* him. Maybe just as desperately as he needs me. If I am here, I might as well enjoy his cock? *Right?*

I bite my lip, prepared to make a move as soon as he enters, but he seems distracted. I deflate. Usually...he looks at me like I am his whole world. Like I am the best part of his day. But this time, he doesn't enter the box right away and kiss me.

"Sorry, baby. I got caught up in work. There is a charity gala tonight, and so much still needs to be done." He stares down at his phone as he talks to me. Charity gala? Tonight? My rose-sex-covered glasses are quickly replaced with the truth. His excuse is a stupid fucking party for even more stupid rich people? I thought...I thought I mattered? It shouldn't hurt, but it does. I am not his equal. I am Kane's toy. Only to be taken out when he gets bored, but the second he has something else to capture his attention, I am going to be stuck in this fucking prison all alone.

I dig my nails into my palms and clench my jaw in anger. I feel a deep sense of betrayal. Worst of all, I feel like an idiot. For the first time since my mother died, I didn't feel so alone, and it turned out to be some sick farce. Kane doesn't care about me; I am just a hobby to him! He is a rich fucking asshole who gets whatever he wants and throws it away the second he gets bored of it.

"Haven?" Kane asks, confused, finally looking up from his phone. "Baby, what's wrong?"

"Why would anything be wrong?" I scoff.

He puts away his phone and flexes his jaw. Well, at least I garnered some of his attention.

"I will ask you one more time. What is the matter?" he bites out.

"Nothing," I drawl.

Kane quickly unlocks the door and stalks into my enclosure. His approach would have intimidated me a week ago, but now I welcome it. *Show me just how big and bad you can be, asshole,* I think to myself. I want to fight. He closes the gap quickly and grabs me by the hips. His touch feels like heaven and hell at the same time. Maybe he is a demon sent to torture me.

"Haven, god damn it. You know I *hate* secrets. Now, do I need to bend you over and spank you until you tell me the truth?" he growls.

I know myself well enough that I can't let that happen. For if I do, I know exactly what it will lead to, and I can't afford to let his cock cloud my judgment.

"Fuck you, Kane!" I bite out, and I can see in his expression that he doesn't expect me to have so much vim. Maybe he thought this was some fun new fore-play, but he is about to be sorely disappointed. "A charity gala? Here? And tell me, do your rich friends know about me being kept imprisoned just below their feet?"

"No..." He falters but grips my hips tighter.

"No? Hmm, funny that."

"Haven—"

"You said you wouldn't leave me alone!" I bellow, and while I am pissed at myself for doing a terrible job of hiding my emotions, I can't help it. "But you did! You never came this morning, and when you did, you didn't even pay attention to me. Now, you are leaving me again to go to some stupid party while I am stuck in *here*," I sob, trying to fight out of his grasp. I can see his expression soften, and I am terrified to hear the sweetly spun excuse he will use to try to manipulate me.

"Baby, look at me. Look"—he grabs my face and I clamp my wet eyes closed—"at me. I am so sorry for not coming earlier. You are right, I was distracted, but that is no excuse. You are the most important thing in the world to me. I will make it up to you, I swear. Whatever you want, baby. It's yours."

My chest tightens, and I try to block out his words, but they only make me cry harder.

"As for the gala, baby, you just aren't..." He sighs and stops to find his words. "Ready."

Not ready? Not...*ready*? Like I am a dog training for a competition. Rage consumes me, and I welcome it. I successfully shove him away from me, and while he fights to regain control, I wind up my hand and fling it forward...

*SMACK.*

I hit him directly across the face, and both of us still. Kane looks at me with utter disbelief. My chest heaves, and I try to steady my breathing. My hand shakes, and I can't even register what transpired between us. Seconds turn into minutes, and I realize I can deliver the fatal blow.

"I will never be ready because I will *never* love you." The lie slips off of my tongue, and for a brief second, it feels good to see him wounded. My words hurt more than the slap. His eyebrows furrow, creating a deep crease in his forehead as he contemplates my words. His arms fall to his sides, and I can see him clenching his fists like he is swaying at sea with no anchor. His eyes desperately search my own for any truth in my statement until they turn cold and unfeeling. His stare mirrors my own after we had sex, absent-minded and numb. I want him to scream at me, command me to tell him it isn't true, and to fuck me like these are our very last moments. But he does none of those things. For the first time since I met him, Kane accepts defeat and makes his way toward the exit. But with every step he takes away from me, I feel like I can't breathe.

I have won a battle, so why does it feel like I've lost? I meet his eyes for what feels like the final time just before the elevator doors close, and only once I am alone do I permit myself to cry.

I crumple to the ground and hold myself as I let the pain wash over me. The grief is unbearable.

"*Meow.*" Luna saunters over to me for comfort.

"Oh, Luna, what have I done?" I cry into her black fur. She purrs against my chest and everything that transpired replays in my mind.

"*I will never be ready because I will never love you.*" I thought if I said it out loud, it would somehow make it true. But it only confirmed that despite my best efforts, I am already in love with Kane Turner.

## CHAPTER 6
# KANE

I shoot back another glass of whiskey.

"I will never be ready because I will never love you." Her words replay in my head, taunting me. I stare at the engagement ring that I had perfectly fitted for Haven earlier today. That's why I was gone. That is why I had left her alone. The jeweler had a few complications earlier today that forced me out of the manor and away from Haven. Now, the ring only serves as an expensive reminder that she doesn't want it. She doesn't want to be my wife. I close the dark red velvet lid on the large diamonds and shove the small box back into my pocket.

I try to pour more amber liquid into my cup but nothing comes out. I raise the empty bottle of Glenfiddich and suddenly feel the need to throw it at the wall.

"Guests, sir," Agatha whispers, reading my mind. She has always been able to sense when things go awry. It has been no surprise to me that she has been at my side all evening.

"How could I forget? They drink my booze, dirty my house, and who decided to play this god-awful music-cc," I slur my words slightly. I'm drunk—no, I am fucking wasted. And while I like to drink, I hate being out of control. Being drunk alone is unusual, but being drunk in front of others at my own party is unprecedented.

"You did, sir," Agatha reminds me.

"Yeah, well. I'm stupid." I begin searching for any kind of alcohol to try and ease the searing pain in my heart as the harpist plays her pretty tunes.

*Haven will never love me.*

*Haven will never love me.*

*Haven will never love me.*

The sentence plays alongside the melody in my head. I just need it to stop. I will do *anything* to make it stop.

"Kane, great party as usual." The chairman on my board of directors, Dave Branson, approaches me and reaches out his hand to shake it. When I don't offer mine in return, he asks, "Is everything alright? You seem...unlike yourself."

No one has the balls to call me out of my behavior outright. I'm wasted at a charity gala; my behavior should be seen as reprehensible, but when you have a billion dollars to your name, you can do whatever you want. I could get into that foundation outside. Just as the thought crosses my mind, I want to test my theory. I stop rummaging through the booze and stumble my way outside.

"Kane?" Dave calls out behind me.

"Sir, please come back inside," Agatha begs as she chases after me, but nothing matters anymore. *I* don't matter anymore. Haven has been my reason for existence ever since my parents died.

I start stripping off my bowtie.

*Now, I will never be able to give her my mother's ring.*

I throw my jacket off to the side.

*She will never give me a child.*

I slide my shoes off and jump into the fountain.

By now, a crowd has gathered. Sharp cold water plasters my face and I embrace the pain. I can't wait to hear the gossip circulate through the press. I wonder which of these rats will supply the first-hand tidbit first. "Billionaire Kane Turner gone mad, what is his drug of choice?" The funniest thing of all is that I will never guess correctly. Coke? No. Speed? No. Ketamine? No. It is the vixen I've stalked for the past four years. Oh, the press would go crazy for that.

I can't help but chuckle. My entire life is one big joke. It feels good to feel something. All of New York City's elites watch on as I have a life crisis. But they don't care. They find it...charming. I hear cheers and laughter surrounding the fountain until a few people join in. I can't stand it. These are the same people who mocked, jeered, and gossiped about my parents. These are the same people who copy everything I do to gain an ounce of my favor. They see me as a way to advance their own status. That is why I have felt alone all of my life. I hate all of these people. But not Haven. She would be able to see my pain if she was here. She *should* be here. I close my eyes and reconcile what must be done.

"Mr. Turner, please. Let me get you dried off and grab you a coffee," Agatha pleads, and I look at her. "It will be alright, sir."

"No." I shake my head. "No, it won't."

Dave approaches Agatha to what I can only imagine is to inquire about my current state. I can't hear what they are saying, but he appears frustrated. To hell with him and to hell with everyone here.

"Everyone get out," I say, but only a few people hear me. "I said, GET OUT!" I scream and pull myself out of the fountain. My guests look at me with fear and concern. What they thought was a fun twist in their evening has now turned sour.

"Get them out, Agatha," I command.

"Of course, sir." She and the other servants go straight to work, ushering people out of the manor.

"Have you lost your mind?" Dave bites out, following my wet trail.

"Watch your mouth, Dave." I stop abruptly and pull out the last ounce of authority from my drunken state. "You might be the head of directors, but I will see you fired in an instant."

Dave clamps his mouth shut. I'll deal with the board on Monday. But right now, I have more important matters to attend to.

THE ELEVATOR DOORS open to the bunker, and my arrival appears to wake Haven. My clothes are drenched, and I am being tormented by the sound of their incessant dripping.

*Drip.*

*Drip.*

*Drip.*

I don't have much time until the alcohol completely

consumes me, so it is imperative that I get straight to the point. If Haven has any chance of leaving, this will be it. Sober me is too weak and too obsessive to do it. But drunk me can give her this chance. They say if you love something, set it free. So why don't I want that? I sure as fuck love her with my entire being. Why does this feel like I am ripping my heart out? I don't want Haven to be free; I want her to be *mine*. The only problem is, she doesn't want that. Despite my best efforts, Haven Mathews still hates me.

I unlock the door to her box, and she quickly stands.

"Kane? What happened? Why are you wet—"

I cut off her concern with a passionate kiss. My mouth encases her own, and I make sure to take my time enjoying her as it will be my last. She initially meets my kiss with surprise but then with equal enthusiasm. My hands cup her face, and I let my tongue explore her mouth. She lets out a gentle moan that I fear will unravel me. I contemplate trashing my brief moment of sanity to take her upstairs, forcing her orgasm over and over again.

I compel myself to break our separation and take in her beautiful face. Her eyes are red and puffy. She must have been crying....all alone. I close my eyes in shame. I've become the monster she claimed me to be.

"Kane, you are scaring me. How much have you had

to drink?" she asks, and her voice is so gentle it almost sounds like she cares. My vision starts to darken, and I can feel my body begin to sway. Haven grasps my wet tuxedo shirt to stabilize me, but eventually, she opts to let me lay in her bed on the floor.

"I am letting you go," I whisper.

"What?" she asks in disbelief.

"You can go." I feel acid rising in my throat. "Go, Haven. Because the second I sober up, I will not spare any expense to track you back down. Go and go far. To someplace even I can't find you. That will be the only way you will be truly free because god only knows I cannot be. You are the air that I breathe, Haven. My only reason to exist. I know I kept you in this god-awful box, and for that, I will be forever sorry. But this is how my soul feels. You might have been my prisoner, but you are the captor of my heart. You will *never* love me, but I will *always* love you. I now know that is my punishment for my crimes against you."

I hear her mumbling something in response, but I am too far gone to comprehend what she is saying. My hearing is officially muffled as I watch her moving mouth multiply around me. It is like I am surrounded by three Havens. Three angels.

I raise my hand and caress her cheek as the blackness creeps in. My eyes start to flutter shut, and I pray I can enjoy this last moment of peace. For in the morning, I will be a changed man. A desperate and angry man. I embrace the darkness, hoping I never wake up to my new reality.

## CHAPTER 7
# HAVEN

I didn't expect Kane to return tonight. Imagine my surprise when he showed up reeking of whiskey and declaring I could leave. I look down at his unconscious body, which is drenched with water. What the hell did he do? Despite my anger, sadness, and frustration, I can't help but worry about him. Although I haven't known him for long, it is more than evident that he is a man who doesn't like to be out of control.

I look towards the unlocked door of my prison. I am only a few steps and an elevator ride away from my freedom. I should feel much better about my predicament, but I let out an uneasy breath and pinch the bridge of my nose. I look back down towards Kane, and I can observe him unabashedly for the first time. His pale skin with high cheekbones is both feminine and masculine in harmony. It's like he was sculpted by a god. My eyes travel downward, and his soaked tuxedo shirt perfectly outlines his abs. I brush my hand across them and can confirm that they are indeed rock solid. I guess he has a hobby other than just stalking me. A gentle smirk grows across my face until my eye catches a soft light emanating from his pant pocket.

It's the first time I've looked down below his waist, which is a surprise, considering I've spent the majority of the past few days drooling over his persistent bulge. Weird, his wet trousers showcase two perfectly outlined items in his pockets. One is obviously his cell phone, which I reach in to grab, but the other is a...

My hand stills the second I feel the velvet casing. My heart begins frantically pounding as I slowly pull out the small box.

It can't be.

It *is*.

"Fuck," I whisper as I stare at a gorgeous red velvet ring box. My hands shake, but I force myself to look inside. I know what to expect, but it's still a shock nonetheless. I let out an audible gasp at the sight of the most beautiful engagement ring I have ever seen. This can't be for me, can it? Who the fuck else would it be for?

Although I know I shouldn't, I pluck it out from the mini cushion and slide it onto my finger. It's a perfect fit. I hold out my hand and observe the diamonds' glitter under the sterile box lighting. This had to have cost a fortune. I ogle at the ring's beauty until I am pulled out of my trance when Kane's phone lights up again.

"Jesus Christ," I exclaim as I look down at his phone screen. He has over twenty messages from all kinds of people, but I can't read them all. His phone is locked. Go figure. I take a wild guess and type in my birthday. BINGO! A week ago, I would have thought it was so fucking creeping, but now I find it ridiculously endearing. Kane isn't as slick as he thinks he is.

I know I shouldn't, but I start rummaging around his text messages. I want more insight into the man who keeps his cards close to his chest. What spurred his sudden change of heart? Why does he want me to leave but still carry this ring in his pocket?

*Jack (Marketing): When will you be back in the office?*

*Larry (Board member): Hello, Mr. Turner; we have not seen you at the recent board meeting. Do you plan to attend the next?*

*Dave pain-in-my-ass Branson: Kane, there is a crisis.*

*Axel Warren (Fuck face socialite): Mr. Turner, we want to donate to the Turner Foundation.*

MY GOD, it just keeps going and going. Every contact has a funny names or title, undoubtedly a method to help him manage the multitude of individuals making demands of him. And to think, he hadn't even looked at his phone when he was with me. I think back to our interaction earlier, and guilt starts consuming me. But still, he can't just leave me in this prison when he goes off and parties. I'm not a pet—

Every justification in my mind cuts off when I see the contact name "Charles (Jeweler)." I immediately click on the message chain, and my heart sinks to my stomach.

*Charles: Mr. Turner, the ring is in superb condition. However, we've run into some snags with the band size adjustment. It would be best if you could come into the shop so we can discuss our options further.*

I IMMEDIATELY TOUCH my fingers to find them bare. Suddenly, the memory of him taking them off before my bath comes to mind.

*Kane: What issues exactly? I've decided to move my plans for the proposal up to tonight. Can this not be resolved over the phone? As always, any priority service charge can be added directly to my tab.*

*Charles: I am afraid not, sir. Considering how old the ring is and that it belonged to the late Mrs. Turner, it is imperative that you come in personally.*

*Kane: I understand. I will stop by shortly.*

*Charles: See you soon!*
*Charles: Thank you for stopping by today, Mr. Turner. And as always, we appreciate the mighty generous tip you left. Cheers to you. Just to confirm, we have opened a new tab for Haven Turner. Our staff cannot wait to meet her and pick out any pieces she might want for the wedding.*

I FEEL like I am going to be sick.

Mother's ring. New tab. Proposal. Tonight.

My head is spinning with a million thoughts. This is why he was gone. He was getting his dead mother's ring fitted for me so that he could propose. Then he went and opened a tab for me so I could shop? This is why he was on his phone. All of the events that took place earlier in the day start clicking into place.

I fall back on my ass and sit in sheer disbelief. How could I be so wrong?

"*Meowwww.*" Luna saunters over to Kane's unmoving body, headbutting him for attention.

I need air. I need to fucking breathe. I rip off the undeserved engagement ring, shoving it back into the box, and grab Luna. For the first time in a week, I freely step out of my prison and make my way to the elevator. When the doors close, I feel my legs give out from underneath me. I slide down the wall and hold Luna in my arms. Even the ornate elevator makes me feel so small, so ignoble.

The elevator stops at what appears to be the ground floor. Wait, what if the party is still going on? Shit, shit, shit!

I try hitting as many buttons as possible to prevent the doors from opening, but it is too late. I brace myself for total embarrassment, but I am met with dead silence and the remnants of a party. I guess it ended early. I take a few hesitant steps out of the elevator in nothing but Kane's dress shirt and my fluffy black cat. It must be quite a sight to see in such a grand manor. All of a sudden, a great noise echos in the hall

*Bong.*

*Bong.*

*Bong.*

A massive grandfather clock chimes, nearly frightening Luna and me half to death. My poor kitty digs her nails into my shoulder. It seems like the sound is coming from one of the towers. I shake my head and scoff. This place cannot be real. There appear to be a few servants cleaning up leftover drinks and food, but none of them acknowledge my existence. I then see Agatha fishing out clothing from the fountain outside. Other than Kane, she is the only familiar face to me. I take a few brisk steps and push open two glass doors that lead outside.

"Ah. So this must be why he is soaking wet," I interrupt her

"Miss Mathews." She nods her head in respect. I am not used to that kind of treatment.

"Please just call me Haven," I implore her

"Unfortunately, miss, that is not how things are done here at the Turner Manor," she says matter-of-factly.

Well, okay then.

"How is he?" she asks, and it is clear she is breaking one of her own rules.

"Not good," I answer honestly. "He set me free."

"I can see that."

A few moments pass, and neither of us knows what to say until Agatha finally breaks the silence. "This will kill him."

"What?" Her words rattle me.

"Kane has never been a normal boy. Not ever since he was a baby. Perhaps that's why he attached himself from that day of his parents' funeral. But despite his... idiosyncrasies, he treats people very well. He loves fiercely, and he is unnaturally loyal."

"But he shouldn't love me. I shouldn't love him." I try to speak rationally despite feeling the opposite.

"I know you two had a...unconventional start. But ask yourself, have your feelings for him changed?" Agatha proposes the question.

"Of course they have," I confess.

"And yet you still contemplate leaving?"

"I don't deserve him." Tears start welling in my eyes as I admit my feelings out loud, "I don't deserve his mother's ring. I don't deserve any of this."

"It is because you don't think you deserve it that just proves that you do. Kane is not perfect; god knows he has his fair share of issues. If there was some kind of misunderstanding between the two of you, it would be understandable. Don't beat yourself up about it."

I didn't realize I needed to hear those words. Without realizing it, I wanted someone to give me permission to accept my circumstances. According to society, I should be appalled by Kane's behavior, and in the beginning, I was. But now...everything is different. Now, I crave him just as much as he craves me.

I look at Agatha and take in her gentle face. Her wrinkles perfectly complement her graying hair. She gives me a soft, understanding smile, and I realize how much I miss my mother. I miss not being alone.

"*Purrrrr.*" Luna rests her little head on my shoulder and is content in my arms. I remember all the years we've spent together. It was just me and her. A lonely girl with her cat. But even she has someone else. Unknown to me, she had Kane. It's time I did, too.

I look around the manor, and it's bigger than I could imagine.

"Agatha, is it possible for you to give us a tour?"

"Of course, miss."

We start in the gardens, and I imagine it will take us the rest of the night to explore every part of the manor. But for the first time in a long time, I feel a sense of belonging. It is a foreign emotion I don't quite under-stand how to describe until it hits me: I feel at home.

# CHAPTER 8
# KANE

I peel open one of my eyes. The light above me is like a thousand suns, and my brain feels like it's about to explode.

"Fuck," I groan, trying to regain control of my senses. What the fuck did I do last night? Bits of memories start returning to me in flashes. The fountain. The drinking. The...ring. Fuck, Haven. I jolt awake and sit up so quickly that I fear I might vomit. I am in her enclosure...but where the fuck is she?

It takes me a minute to remember what I said and did. *Kane, you fucking idiot!* Grief and rage start to consume my heart. But it all comes to a boiling point when I recognize the small velvet box and my phone sitting on the ground. She found my mother's ring. I grab it frantically in hopes that it may be gone. But instead, it is placed perfectly in its cushion. My breathing intensifies, and as I shove the box back into my pocket, I glance around to find Luna missing. Of course, she wouldn't leave without her. That confirms it. She is gone, and I fucking let her go.

I rise to my feet and let the hangover assault me. I don't fucking care. I only feel rage and anguish. I hurl my phone at the glass wall, which smashes it to bits, reflecting the scars of my heart. I grab a nearby chair and use it to smash the computer monitor screens. The room transforms into chaos, and pieces of equipment I've used to watch her for years fly everywhere. My breath is guttural and primal, and I let out a scream that resembles that of a wounded animal. Why did I let her go? Why did she leave? Fuck fuck *fuck!*

The smashing only amplifies as I continue to wreak havoc on the space. But a sudden punctuating ding reverberates through the air.

"God damn it, Agatha. You know better than to interrupt me at a time like this—" My words are cut short as I take in the female presence before me.

"Haven..." I whisper her name like a prayer. I can't believe my eyes. I must have truly lost my mind.

"I brought you breakfast. Your favorite...eggs and bacon," she says sweetly and stares at me with her big doe eyes with her hair in a messy bun. She could make any grown man fall to his knees, so that is precisely what I do.

Please be real. Please be real.

"Please tell me you are real," I plead.

Haven sets the breakfast tray on one of the trashed tables and walks over to me. She cups my face in her hands and a rogue tear rolls down my cheeks. I haven't cried since my parents died.

"As real as can be," she reassures me. "Hey, look at me."

I pry open my eyes and look into her beautiful face. "You came back," I croak.

"I will never leave you. *Never*," she repeats the words I said to her in the bath. I let out a ragged breath, and I feel like some part of my soul has been set free.

"I'm not sure you know what you've done. Now that you have me, you'll have a hell of a time getting rid of me."

"Never," I growl and grab her hips, lifting her as I stand so she cradles my waist.

She squeals, but I silence her with my mouth. We kiss like we've been starved of each other for eternity. Fuck, I can't get enough of her. I carry her towards the elevator; I need out of this pit in the ground, and so does she. Never again will she be trapped down here.

"I am sorry, baby. I'm so sorry!" I apologize

profusely between kisses, and my raging boner pokes into her wet panties. Those are going to smell so fucking good.

"Mmm, no, I'm sorry. I didn't know you were fixing your mother's ring." She grinds against my dick, but I'm not yet too far gone that I don't pick apart her words. Fix? The only way she would know I was at the jeweler was if she...went through my phone. The realization hits me: my girl is also a snooper. Pride swells in my chest. But I use this as an excuse to enforce some kind of punishment.

Haven sucks on my tongue and moans into my mouth as I grab the elevator's emergency brake.

"Wha-what just happened?" she asks in a daze.

"How did you know where I went?"

"Huh?"

"You heard me? How did you know I went to...fix the ring, which, by the way, you could have only discovered by going through my pockets when I was passed out?"

"Ahh uh...umm...I may have gone through your texts."

"Hmm. And how precisely did you do that?" I was genuinely curious.

"I guessed that your phone password was my birthday, and what do you know? I was right." She lets out a nervous laugh and bites her bottom lip. "Are you mad?"

she asks with a hint of fear in her eyes. It would seem she is desperate to please me. My sweet girl.

"Not mad, but I think you must be punished for spoiling the surprise."

"Punished, how?"

"Get on all fours." I place her down on the elevator floor. When she assumes the position, I lift the dress shirt to find lace thong panties and an exposed ass. I wind my hand back...

*SMACK.*

"Ah!" she screams

*SMACK.*

"Fuck!" she grunts.

"That's it, baby. Take your punishment like a good girl."

"I'm sorry—" *SMACK.* "Ahhh!"

"Sorry for what? Say it."

*SMACK.*

"I'm sorry for ruining the surprise!"

*SMACK.* Her bottom is beet red with my handprint. Almost like I've branded her, and in a way, I have. She is mine and mine forever.

"I'm sorry for leaving. I'm sorry for fighting with you. I'm sorry for not seeing sooner how much you love me," she screams out all of her regrets as if this spanking is some kind of penance. Her words make me feel like my cock is about to explode, and she hasn't even touched me. But I have to make sure she has no need to apologize.

"Shh, baby. You aren't being punished for those things." Still, I take the opportunity to give her one final spank.

*SMACK.*

"Mmm," she moans, and I can see the pain quickly turning to pleasure.

"Oh, you like that, don't you? You dirty little slut. I bet if I flip a finger into these panties, I'm going to find a soaking wet pussy, aren't I?"

"Mhmm." She nods her head fervently.

So I do just that. I dip my finger, and her pussy is dripping.

"Fuck, Haven. Your cunt is so wet," I growl. I've waited fucking days for this. I pull my finger back to my mouth and taste her juice. So fucking delicious.

"Do you want to taste yourself?" I ask.

"I do," she whines.

I go in for a second and slide two fingers into her, ensuring they are perfectly coated.

"Fuck!" she moans, and I bring them up to her mouth. She sticks out her tongue and begins sucking. "Mmmmm, I *do* taste good."

I feel like I'm going to combust, but I remember the

promise I made to myself. I wasn't going to fuck Haven until she begged me to.

I pull back suddenly and leave her desperate for more.

"What the hell?" she cries.

"Do you want more?" I ask matter-of-factly.

"Well...duh!" She sits back on her legs and looks at me confused.

"Then beg."

She flattens her lips and squints her eyes at me with a challenge. Ohhhh, this is going to be fun.

"You want me...to beg when your cock feels like this?" She runs her hands over my raging boner, and I flinch under the touch. Haven starts unzipping my pants, and my dick flings forth, throbbing. At this point, I haven't come in days. I don't think I could if I tried. Her pussy has ruined me forever.

She leans forward and gives the head of my dick a quick lick.

"Fuck!" I moan, and my head falls back. God damn it, this woman holds so much power over me.

"Oh, you like that? Do you want more," she teases, but no matter how much she tries. Unfortunately for her, she is at a disadvantage. On the other hand, I know what it's like to wait years to get what I want.

She dips her head back down and slides my shaft all

the way to the back of her throat. I push on her head to encourage her to take more and more...and more.

She gags and comes back up for air.

"Good girl. You took so much," I praise her.

"Mhm, but I can take more," she promises and returns to my cock. Her head starts bobbing up and down until she starts rhythmically sucking my dick. With every stroke, she gets deeper until her nose hits the base of my shaft.

"Fuck, just like that, baby! Yes, yes!" She loves my encouragement, and I can see her pussy start dripping on the elevator floor.

"I need you! Fuck, I need you so bad, baby." Haven comes up for air pleading with me. That's what I like to hear.

"Say it." I shove her back on my dick. "Beg for my cock!"

"I need your co-ck so fu-cking bad," she mumbles with her mouth full. "Please!" she cries.

I can't stand it anymore. I need her. I pull her forward so she straddles me. Once she is perfectly aligned, I drive my dick deep into her pussy.

"Yes!" she screams. "You are so fucking deep."

"That's right, baby, take all of me." I pound into her cervix, and I can feel her muscles contracting.

"Fuck, baby! I'm so close," she grunts.

"Yeah? Are you going to come for me?"

"Yes! Yes!" Her cries only encourage me to thrust into her harder and faster. Her pussy clenches around my throbbing cock, and I feel myself growing closer to blowing my load inside of her.

"God, Haven, you are so perfect." I rip off the shirt, and the buttons fly everywhere, exposing her breasts. I dive in for her nipples and start sucking, which sends her over the edge.

"I'm coming!" I thrash erratically into her and start shooting my hot white seed into her.

"Come inside me, yes! Breed me, Kane. I want to have your babies so badly!"

"Shit!" I push her down on my cock and completely empty my balls deep inside her womb.

She collapses onto my chest, and I hold her. Our ragged breathing mingles, and she nuzzles her face into my chest.

"I love you, Kane," she whispers, and I know what true happiness feels like for the first time in my life.

"BABY, STOP! I'M TICKLISH," Haven squeals as I lick her leg under the dark silk covers. We have spent the entire day ravishing each other all across the manor. The hallway, elevator, bathtub. I fear we won't stop until we consume each other.

I kiss up Haven's bare skin as she squirms under my touch. I pass over her pussy for the first time today. If I stop, I won't come back out for a while. And right now, I have a very important question to ask her. I can feel her heat and wetness radiating from her core, tempting me. I love how her body responds to me.

I lay gentle kisses on her tummy all the way up to her breasts. I lap at her nipple and give it a little nibble.

"Mmm," Haven moans and rubs her fingers through my hair.

I practically pry myself off of her tits. I pride myself on my self-control, but she completely unravels me. I finally reach the top of the sheets and embrace the fresh gust of oxygen. I stare up at Haven's beautiful eyes, and she looks at me like I had always hoped. This is it. I raise my hand, holding onto the red velvet box, and she gasps. I flip open the top, and before I can ask the question, she answers.

"Yes!" she screams and grabs my face to plant a deep kiss on my lips.

"I haven't even asked the question!" I feign offense and laugh.

"Oh, sorry." She flings her hand over her mouth and bites her lip.

"Haven Mathews, will you marry me?"

"Yes," she whispers.

"Good, because you don't have a choice," I growl and flip her on top of me.

"Mmm, good to know," Haven purrs and grinds her pussy into my cock, "and you have no choice but to fuck me."

"With pleasure, my love." I brush my lips against hers and start tending to my job diligently. There might be something twisted inside of me but with Haven, I am the happiest man in the world.

# EPILOGUE: HAVEN

*DING.*

The elevator arrives on the third floor, and shopping bag straps from various Fifth Avenue stores dig into my arm. Agatha insists on letting one of the servants carry my stuff, but I'd rather do it myself. There isn't a better feeling than lugging your newly made purchases home and pouring it all out on your bed. Besides, this time, I have a special surprise for Kane.

"*MEOW*." Luna runs up to greet me and rubs her fluffy body along my leg.

"Hi, girly! Miss me?"

"*MROW*," she responds. I will take that as a yes. She stretches out her long body after a few hours of sleeping.

"Oh, it's such a hard life, isn't it?" I mock and bend

83

down to scratch behind her ear. Luna adjusted to our new home quicker than I did. Even if I did decide to leave, she would have wanted to stay behind. Not that I blame her.

"You didn't mention you would be stopping at Tiffany and Co.," Kane grills me as soon as I enter our bedroom.

"Don't you have work to do?" I smile and roll my eyes. I knew that this would happen. In fact, I was counting on it.

"Not when my wife decides to go somewhere without telling me." Kane approaches me, and I'm still not used to his size despite it being a year since he captured me.

"You know I *hate* secrets." Kane tenses his jaw and fidgets with his gold wedding band. I can tell he is anxious. He expects me to tell him the exact stores I intend to shop at so he can have ample time to hack into their security cameras. Old habits die hard.

Kane and I got married in an intimate ceremony soon after he proposed. Funny enough, once I became his under the law, it was like he became more nervous that he would lose me. Not because I would leave but more like something would happen to me. Although he won't admit it, I know it's because of his parents. Because of that, I like to humor him. And I can't lie; I find his overprotectiveness very sexy. Consequently, I rarely do something without his knowledge. But if I am ever going to surprise the bastard, sometimes the rules must be broken.

"Relax, baby. I was just getting you a present." I cup his face, and he nuzzles into my neck.

"I hate when I can't see you. I worry about you." He places a few gentle kisses on my jaw and works his way up to my lips. He grabs my neck with his hand and squeezes tightly. The sensation makes my panties moisten.

"Baby, I have..."—he silences my words with his deep kiss—"to get ready for the gala tonight," I finish my sentence.

"Forget the gala. I *need* you," he moans into my mouth, and I can't help but chuckle. He is acting like I had a near-death experience, but I just went shopping.

"No, baby, the Turner Charity Foundation promised to host a gala. Since I am the president of said organization, it is kind of important that I am there. That we are both there." I decided to take over the Charity Foundation and quit my job when the press kept hounding me in my office. It was impossible to get anything done, and it made for a circus. I could have sworn Kane was about to kill someone. I was initially sad to be leaving, but I have found my new position much more rewarding.

Kane groans, "I can have a chat with your boss. I think he can be persuaded to let you miss one event."

I smack him on the shoulder. "You are terrible."

"Yes, I am," he growls and picks me up.

"Kane!" I squeal.

"No, no, no, you aren't going anywhere until you get your punishment." He throws me on the bed and starts tickling me. I scream with laughter and try to get away from his torturous fingers.

"Okay, okay! You win! Let me at least give you your present." I try to catch my breath after my fit of laughter.

"Haven, we've been over this. *You* are my present. You don't need to get me anything," Kane coos and returns to kissing my neck.

"But I think you are really going to like this one!" I shove him off, and he looks so offended by the rejection that I smile. He is so dramatic.

I jump off the bed and sprint over to one of my many bags. Reaching into the turquoise Tiffany bag, I pull out a velvet bracelet box.

"Here." I shove it toward him with the biggest smile on my face. I can't contain my excitement.

"Okay." He humors me and takes the box from my hand. "If this is their new watch—"

He opens the box, and his words are cut short. Inside is no piece of jewelry or watch. It's a positive pregnancy test.

"Surprise," I whisper as he stares like he can't believe his eyes. I am almost as shocked that he really has no idea. I give myself a mental pat on the back. Getting a pregnancy test without him knowing was like smuggling in illegal contraband to Alcatraz.

"You're pregnant?" He looks up at me with tears welling in his eyes, and I feel myself melt into a pile of mush. We've been trying the entire year to fall pregnant with no luck. I was starting to worry something was wrong until *BAM*. One morning, I cried at the sight of Luna licking herself just because I loved her so much. I didn't want to tell Kane just in case it was a false alarm, so Agatha and I devised a plan. The woman has practically become my partner in crime.

I nod my head fervently, and his stillness turns into pure excitement. I let out another scream as he picks me up and spins me around.

"I'm going to be a dad?" he laughs.

"Yes!" His joy makes me love him even more, which I didn't think was possible. He places me down but doesn't let me go. I thought being his wife made him protective, but now that I am carrying our child, it's going to be a hundred times worse. Lord, help me.

He brings me in for a deep kiss and lets his tears roll freely down his face. "Fuck, baby, I love you so goddamn much."

"I love you too." I sink into his embrace as he caresses my belly.

"But you know...I will love you, if we have a baby or not." He chooses his words carefully, and now it's my turn to cry. I never felt pressure from him to make an heir, but it was always in the gossip tabloids. After a year of failing to conceive, I started feeling like a failure. Hearing those words feels like coming up for a breath of fresh air. I know that as long as I have him, I will be okay.

"I will never leave you. *Never*," he whispers. Those words have become the motto of our relationship.

"Nor I," I whisper back.

Kane growls into my lips, but instead of throwing me back on the bed, he gently lifts me up and lays me down. Ugh, so he wins. I let out a contented sigh as I accept that we will be late to our own party.

# About the Author

Nova Angel is the pen name for spicy monster romance author, K.L. Wyatt. Under this pen name Nova writes short dark(ish) novellas about brutish men.

The love stories written by Nova angel will always include a breeding kink, dark(ish) themes, and happily ever afters.

You can keep up to date with her latest releases+updates when you follow her on instagram or sign-up to her NEWSLETTER.

Made in the USA
Middletown, DE
23 May 2024

54756455R00060